W9-AFP-416

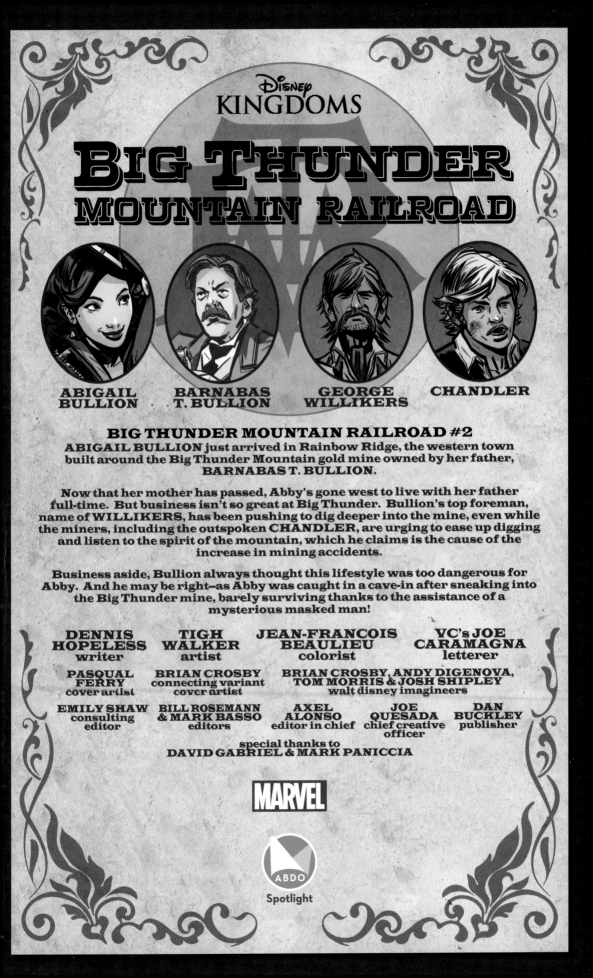

DISNEY KINGDOMS

BIG THUNDER
MOUNTAIN RAILROAD

ABIGAIL BULLION

BARNABAS T. BULLION

GEORGE WILLIKERS

CHANDLER

BIG THUNDER MOUNTAIN RAILROAD #2

ABIGAIL BULLION just arrived in Rainbow Ridge, the western town built around the Big Thunder Mountain gold mine owned by her father, **BARNABAS T. BULLION**.

Now that her mother has passed, Abby's gone west to live with her father full-time. But business isn't so great at Big Thunder. Bullion's top foreman, name of **WILLIKERS**, has been pushing to dig deeper into the mine, even while the miners, including the outspoken **CHANDLER**, are urging to ease up digging and listen to the spirit of the mountain, which he claims is the cause of the increase in mining accidents.

Business aside, Bullion always thought this lifestyle was too dangerous for Abby. And he may be right—as Abby was caught in a cave-in after sneaking into the Big Thunder mine, barely surviving thanks to the assistance of a mysterious masked man!

DENNIS HOPELESS
writer

TIGH WALKER
artist

JEAN-FRANCOIS BEAULIEU
colorist

VC's JOE CARAMAGNA
letterer

PASQUAL FERRY
cover artist

BRIAN CROSBY
connecting variant cover artist

BRIAN CROSBY, ANDY DIGENOVA, TOM MORRIS & JOSH SHIPLEY
walt disney imagineers

EMILY SHAW
consulting editor

BILL ROSEMANN & MARK BASSO
editors

AXEL ALONSO
editor in chief

JOE QUESADA
chief creative officer

DAN BUCKLEY
publisher

special thanks to
DAVID GABRIEL & MARK PANICCIA

MARVEL

ABDO
Spotlight

ABDOPUBLISHING.COM

Reinforced library bound edition published in 2017 by Spotlight,
a division of ABDO, PO Box 398166, Minneapolis, Minnesota 55439.
Spotlight produces high-quality reinforced library bound editions for
schools and libraries. Published by agreement with Marvel Characters, Inc.

Printed in the United States of America, North Mankato, Minnesota.
092016
012017

MARVEL
marvelkids.com
© 2015 MARVEL

**Elements based on Walt Disney's
Big Thunder Mountain Railroad © Disney.**

PUBLISHER'S CATALOGING IN PUBLICATION DATA

Names: Hopeless, Dennis, author. | Walker, Tigh ; Beaulieu, Jean-Francois ; Ruiz, Felix ;
    Mogorron, Guillermo, illustrators.
Title: Big Thunder Mountain Railroad / writer: Dennis Hopeless ; art: Tigh Walker ;
    Jean-Francois Beaulieu ; Felix Ruiz ; Guillermo Mogorron.
Description: Reinforced library bound edition. | Minneapolis, Minnesota : Spotlight, 2017. |
    Series: Disney Kingdoms: Big Thunder Mountain Railroad | Volumes 1, 2 and 4 written by
    Dennis Hopeless ; illustrated by Tigh Walker & Jean-Francois Beaulieu. | Volume 3 written
    by Dennis Hopeless ; illustrated by Felix Ruiz & Jean-Francois Beaulieu. | Volume 5 written
    by Dennis Hopeless ; illustrated by Tigh Walker, Guillermo Mogorron & Jean-Francois
    Beaulieu.
Summary: When Abby traveled west to Rainbow Ridge to live with her father Barnabas T.
    Bullion at the Big Thunder Mountain gold mine, the brave young hero never thought
    she'd join a group of bandits to rob her own father's mine.
Identifiers: LCCN 2016941684 | ISBN 9781614795759 (v.1 ; lib. bdg.) | ISBN 9781614795766
    (v.2 ; lib. bdg.) | ISBN 9781614795773 (v.3 ; lib. bdg.) | ISBN 9781614795780 (v.4 ; lib.
    bdg.) | ISBN 9781614795797 (v.5 ; lib. bdg.)
Subjects: Disney (Fictitious characters)--Juvenile fiction. | Adventures and adventurers--Juvenile
    fiction. | Graphic novels--Juvenile fiction.
Classification: DDC 741.5--dc23
LC record available at https://lccn.loc.gov/2016941684

Spotlight

A Division of ABDO
abdopublishing.com

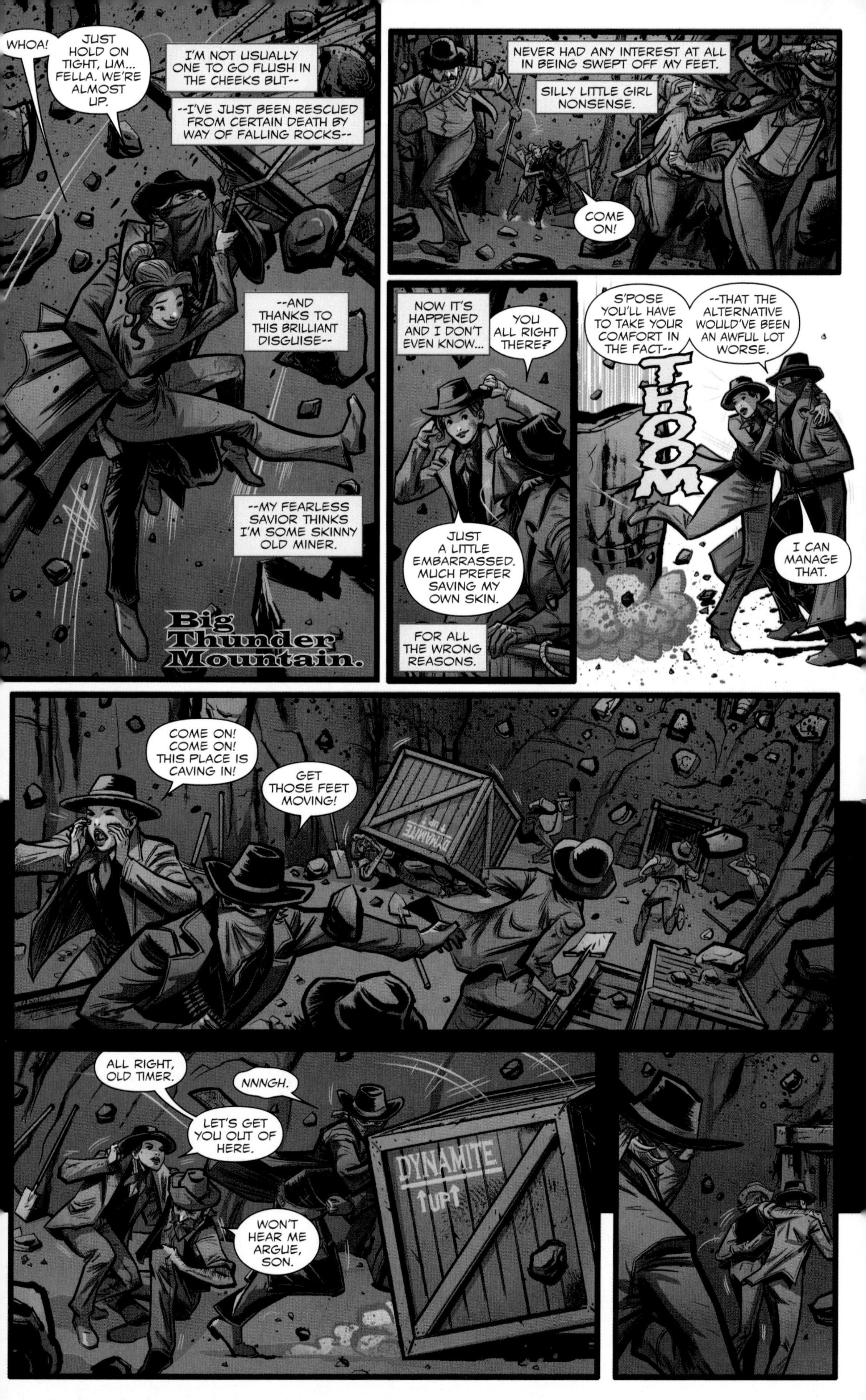
WHOA!
JUST HOLD ON TIGHT, UM... FELLA. WE'RE ALMOST UP.
I'M NOT USUALLY ONE TO GO FLUSH IN THE CHEEKS BUT--
--I'VE JUST BEEN RESCUED FROM CERTAIN DEATH BY WAY OF FALLING ROCKS--
--AND THANKS TO THIS BRILLIANT DISGUISE--
--MY FEARLESS SAVIOR THINKS I'M SOME SKINNY OLD MINER.
Big Thunder Mountain.
NEVER HAD ANY INTEREST AT ALL IN BEING SWEPT OFF MY FEET.
SILLY LITTLE GIRL NONSENSE.
COME ON!
NOW IT'S HAPPENED AND I DON'T EVEN KNOW...
YOU ALL RIGHT THERE?
JUST A LITTLE EMBARRASSED. MUCH PREFER SAVING MY OWN SKIN.
FOR ALL THE WRONG REASONS.
S'POSE YOU'LL HAVE TO TAKE YOUR COMFORT IN THE FACT--
--THAT THE ALTERNATIVE WOULD'VE BEEN AN AWFUL LOT WORSE.
THOOM
I CAN MANAGE THAT.
COME ON! COME ON! THIS PLACE IS CAVING IN!
GET THOSE FEET MOVING!
ALL RIGHT, OLD TIMER.
NNNGH.
LET'S GET YOU OUT OF HERE.
DYNAMITE
UP
WON'T HEAR ME ARGUE, SON.

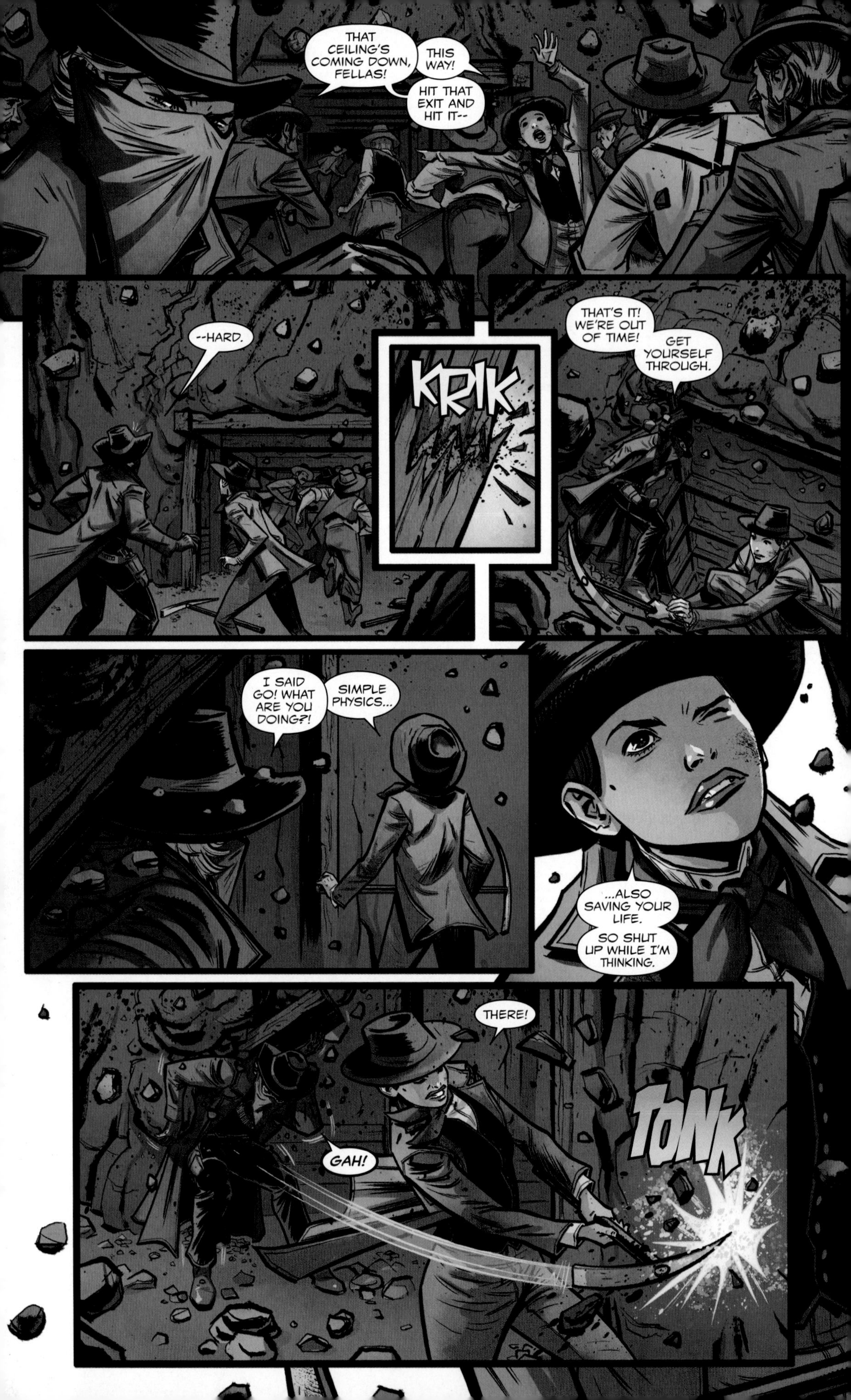
THAT CEILING'S COMING DOWN, FELLAS!
THIS WAY!
HIT THAT EXIT AND HIT IT--
--HARD.
KRIK
THAT'S IT! WE'RE OUT OF TIME!
GET YOURSELF THROUGH.
I SAID GO! WHAT ARE YOU DOING?!
SIMPLE PHYSICS...
...ALSO SAVING YOUR LIFE.
SO SHUT UP WHILE I'M THINKING.
THERE!
GAH!
TONK

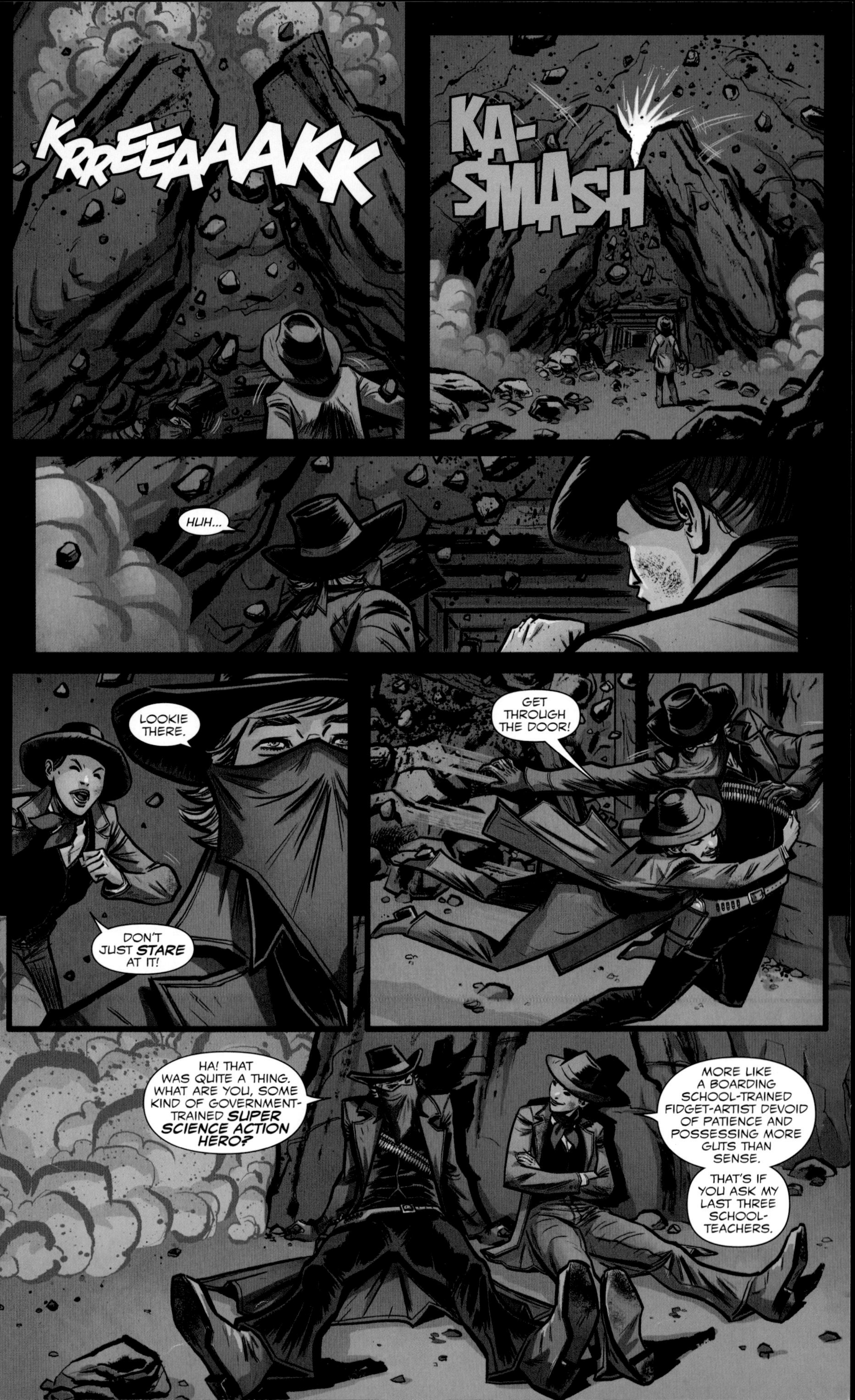
KRREEAAAKK
KA-SMASH
HUH...
LOOKIE THERE.
DON'T JUST STARE AT IT!
GET THROUGH THE DOOR!
HA! THAT WAS QUITE A THING. WHAT ARE YOU, SOME KIND OF GOVERNMENT-TRAINED SUPER SCIENCE ACTION HERO?
MORE LIKE A BOARDING SCHOOL-TRAINED FIDGET-ARTIST DEVOID OF PATIENCE AND POSSESSING MORE GUTS THAN SENSE.
THAT'S IF YOU ASK MY LAST THREE SCHOOL-TEACHERS.

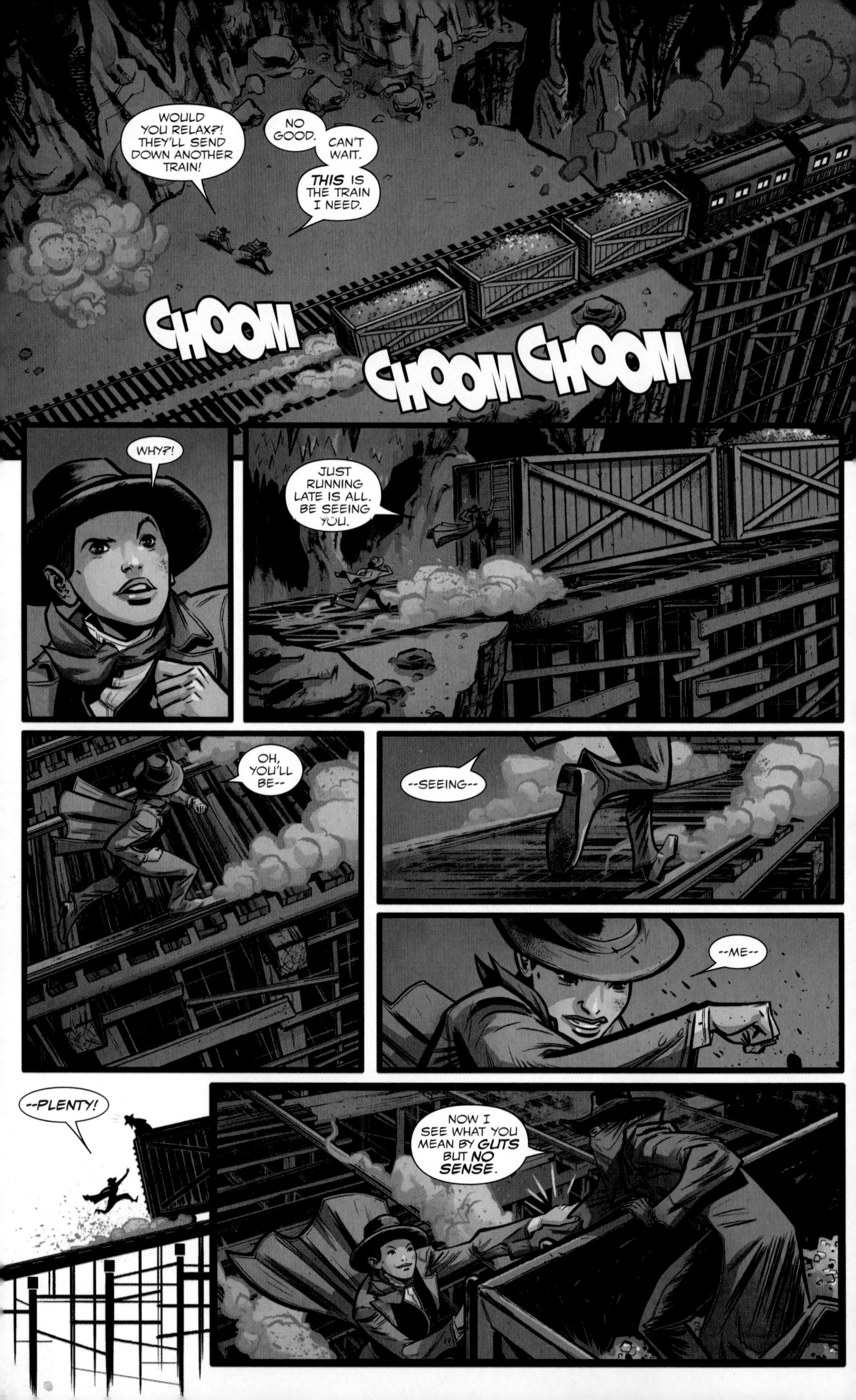
WOULD YOU RELAX?! THEY'LL SEND DOWN ANOTHER TRAIN!
NO GOOD.
CAN'T WAIT.
THIS IS THE TRAIN I NEED.
CHOOM
CHOOM CHOOM
WHY?!
JUST RUNNING LATE IS ALL. BE SEEING YOU.
OH, YOU'LL BE--
--SEEING--
--ME--
--PLENTY!
NOW I SEE WHAT YOU MEAN BY GUTS BUT NO SENSE.

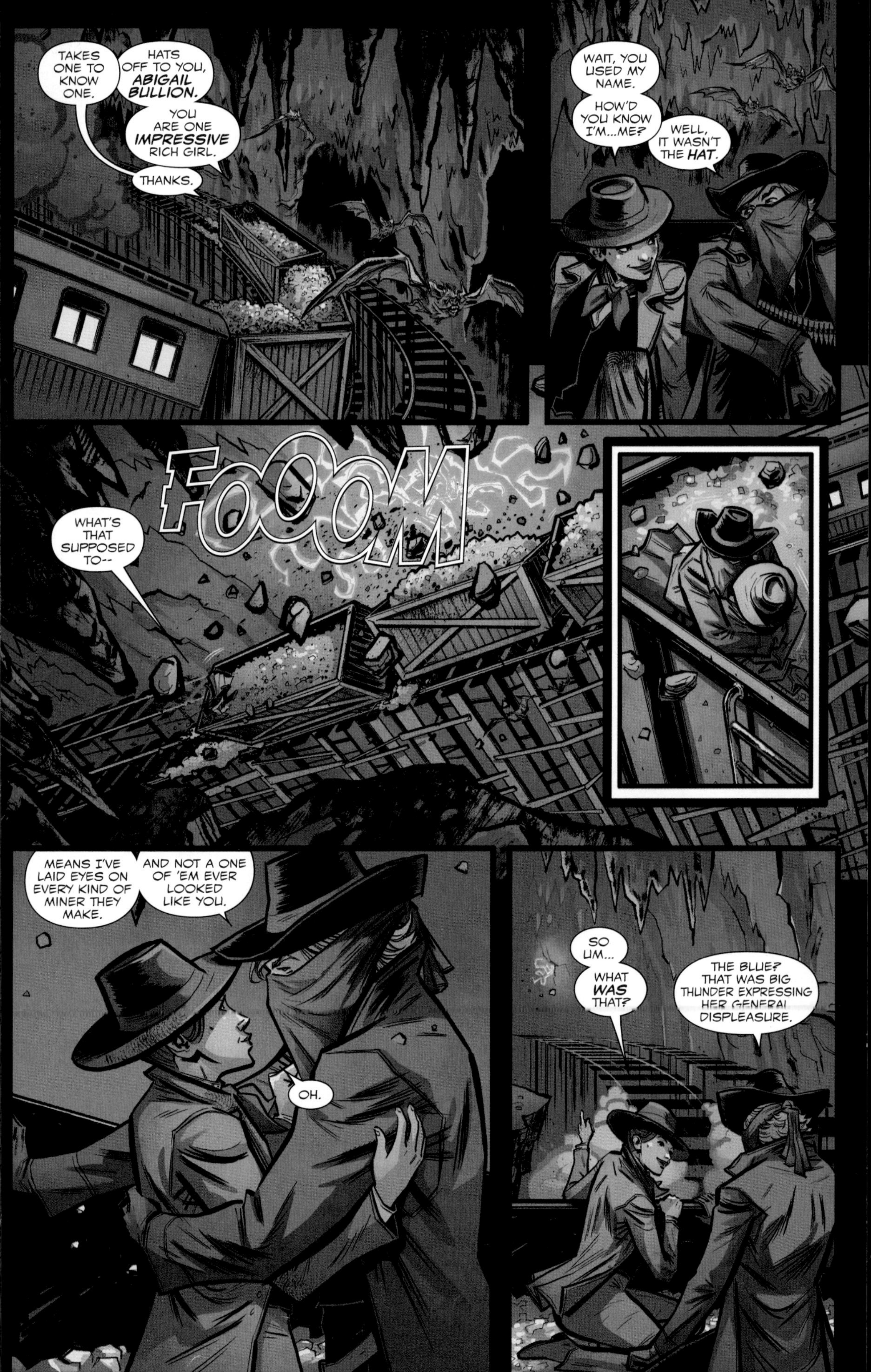

TAKES ONE TO KNOW ONE.
HATS OFF TO YOU, ABIGAIL BULLION.
YOU ARE ONE IMPRESSIVE RICH GIRL.
THANKS.
WAIT, YOU USED MY NAME.
HOW'D YOU KNOW I'M...ME?
WELL, IT WASN'T THE HAT.
FOOOM
WHAT'S THAT SUPPOSED TO--
MEANS I'VE LAID EYES ON EVERY KIND OF MINER THEY MAKE.
AND NOT A ONE OF 'EM EVER LOOKED LIKE YOU.
OH.
SO UM... WHAT WAS THAT?
THE BLUE? THAT WAS BIG THUNDER EXPRESSING HER GENERAL DISPLEASURE.

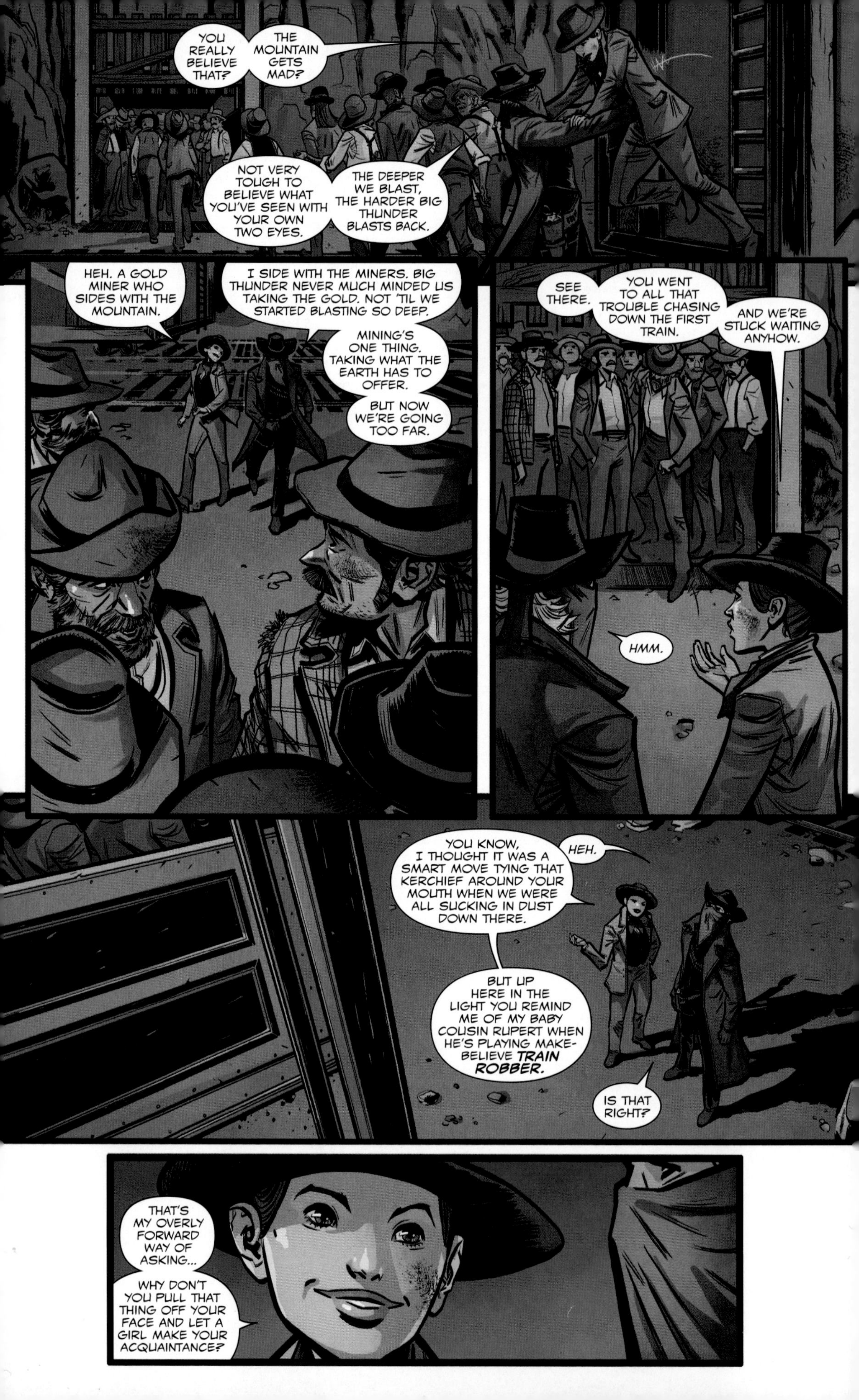

YOU REALLY BELIEVE THAT?
THE MOUNTAIN GETS MAD?
NOT VERY TOUGH TO BELIEVE WHAT YOU'VE SEEN WITH YOUR OWN TWO EYES.
THE DEEPER WE BLAST, THE HARDER BIG THUNDER BLASTS BACK.
HEH. A GOLD MINER WHO SIDES WITH THE MOUNTAIN.
I SIDE WITH THE MINERS. BIG THUNDER NEVER MUCH MINDED US TAKING THE GOLD. NOT 'TIL WE STARTED BLASTING SO DEEP.
MINING'S ONE THING. TAKING WHAT THE EARTH HAS TO OFFER.
BUT NOW WE'RE GOING TOO FAR.
SEE THERE.
YOU WENT TO ALL THAT TROUBLE CHASING DOWN THE FIRST TRAIN.
AND WE'RE STUCK WAITING ANYHOW.
HMM.
YOU KNOW, I THOUGHT IT WAS A SMART MOVE TYING THAT KERCHIEF AROUND YOUR MOUTH WHEN WE WERE ALL SUCKING IN DUST DOWN THERE.
HEH.
BUT UP HERE IN THE LIGHT YOU REMIND ME OF MY BABY COUSIN RUPERT WHEN HE'S PLAYING MAKE-BELIEVE TRAIN ROBBER.
IS THAT RIGHT?
THAT'S MY OVERLY FORWARD WAY OF ASKING...
WHY DON'T YOU PULL THAT THING OFF YOUR FACE AND LET A GIRL MAKE YOUR ACQUAINTANCE?

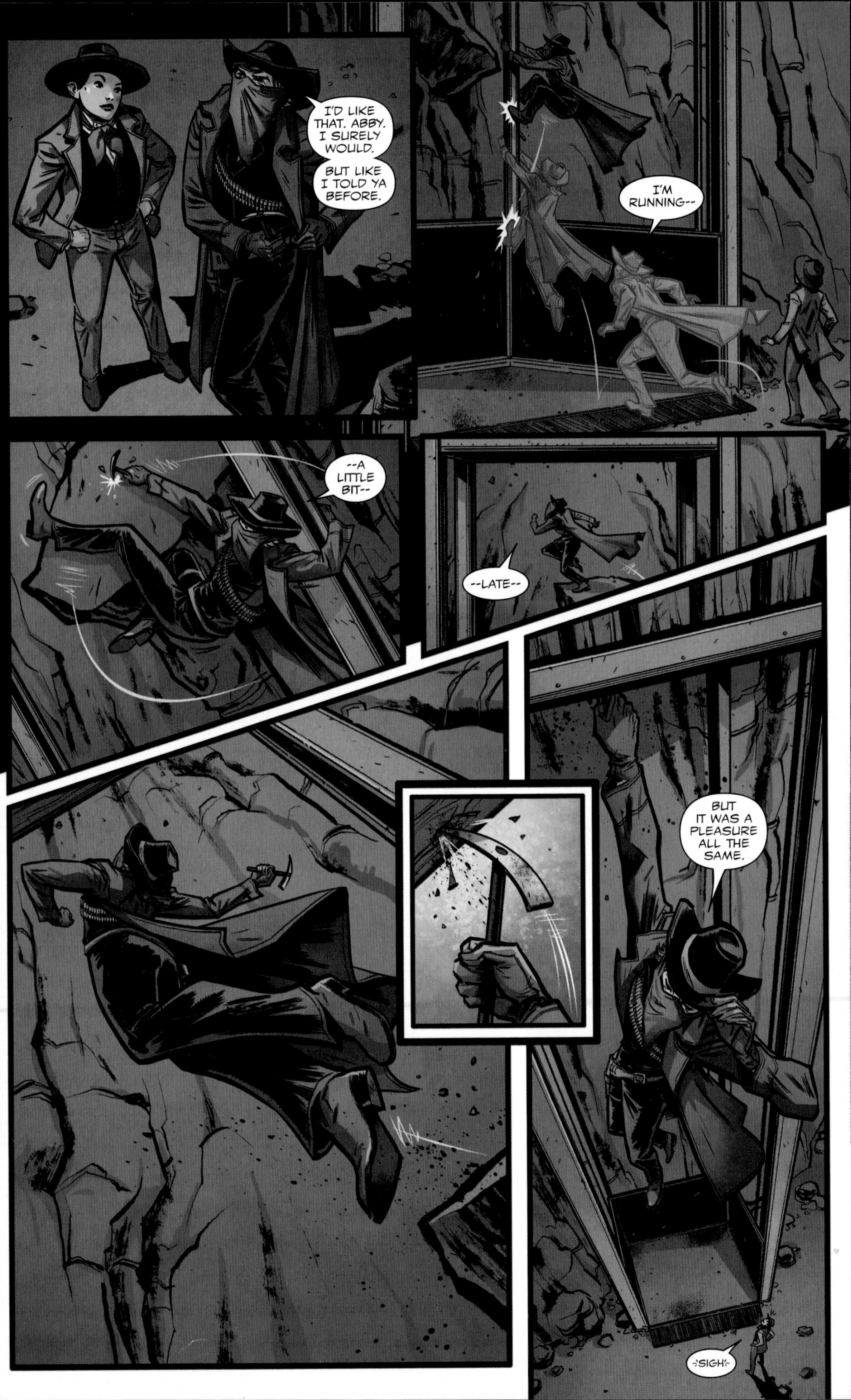
I'D LIKE THAT. ABBY. I SURELY WOULD.
BUT LIKE I TOLD YA BEFORE.
I'M RUNNING--
--A LITTLE BIT--
--LATE--
BUT IT WAS A PLEASURE ALL THE SAME.
SIGH

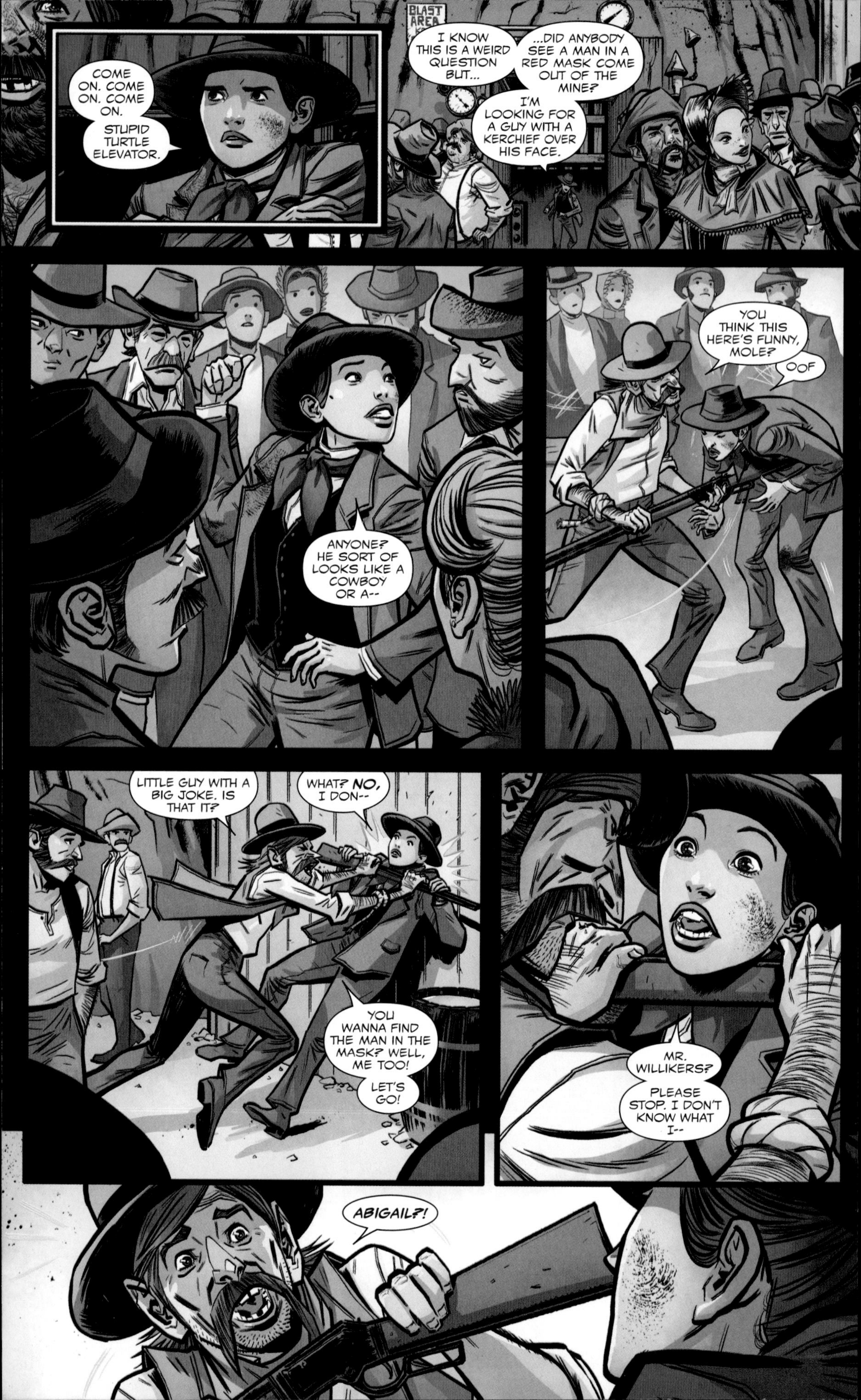
BLAST AREA
COME ON. COME ON. COME ON.
STUPID TURTLE ELEVATOR.
I KNOW THIS IS A WEIRD QUESTION BUT...
...DID ANYBODY SEE A MAN IN A RED MASK COME OUT OF THE MINE?
I'M LOOKING FOR A GUY WITH A KERCHIEF OVER HIS FACE.
ANYONE? HE SORT OF LOOKS LIKE A COWBOY OR A--
YOU THINK THIS HERE'S FUNNY, MOLE?
OOF
LITTLE GUY WITH A BIG JOKE. IS THAT IT?
WHAT? **NO,** I DON--
YOU WANNA FIND THE MAN IN THE MASK? WELL, ME TOO!
LET'S GO!
MR. WILLIKERS?
PLEASE STOP. I DON'T KNOW WHAT I--
ABIGAIL?!

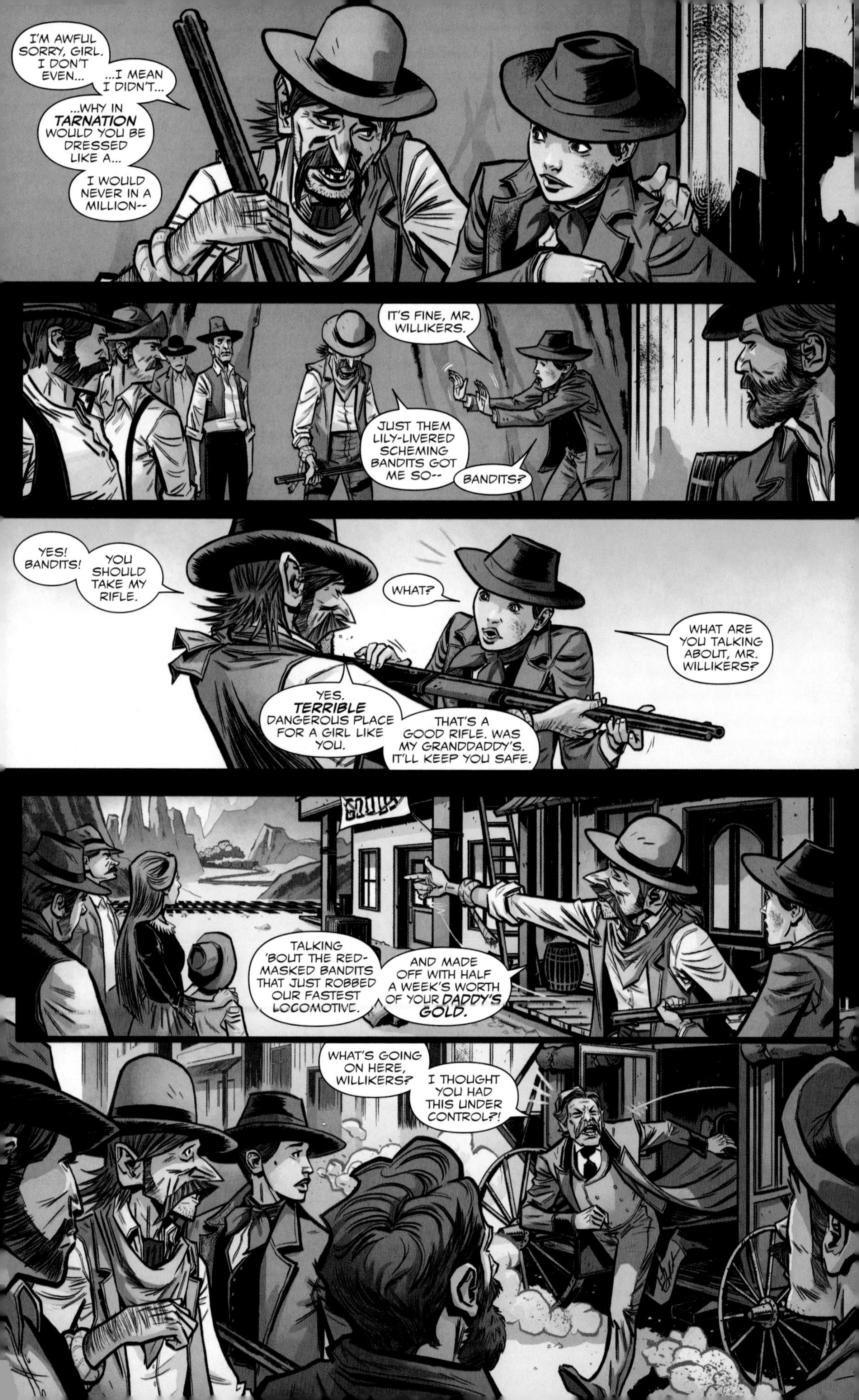
I'M AWFUL SORRY, GIRL. I DON'T EVEN...
...I MEAN I DIDN'T...
...WHY IN TARNATION WOULD YOU BE DRESSED LIKE A...
I WOULD NEVER IN A MILLION--
IT'S FINE, MR. WILLIKERS.
JUST THEM LILY-LIVERED SCHEMING BANDITS GOT ME SO--
BANDITS?
YES! BANDITS!
YOU SHOULD TAKE MY RIFLE.
WHAT?
WHAT ARE YOU TALKING ABOUT, MR. WILLIKERS?
YES. TERRIBLE DANGEROUS PLACE FOR A GIRL LIKE YOU.
THAT'S A GOOD RIFLE. WAS MY GRANDDADDY'S. IT'LL KEEP YOU SAFE.
TALKING 'BOUT THE RED-MASKED BANDITS THAT JUST ROBBED OUR FASTEST LOCOMOTIVE.
AND MADE OFF WITH HALF A WEEK'S WORTH OF YOUR DADDY'S GOLD.
WHAT'S GOING ON HERE, WILLIKERS?
I THOUGHT YOU HAD THIS UNDER CONTROL?!

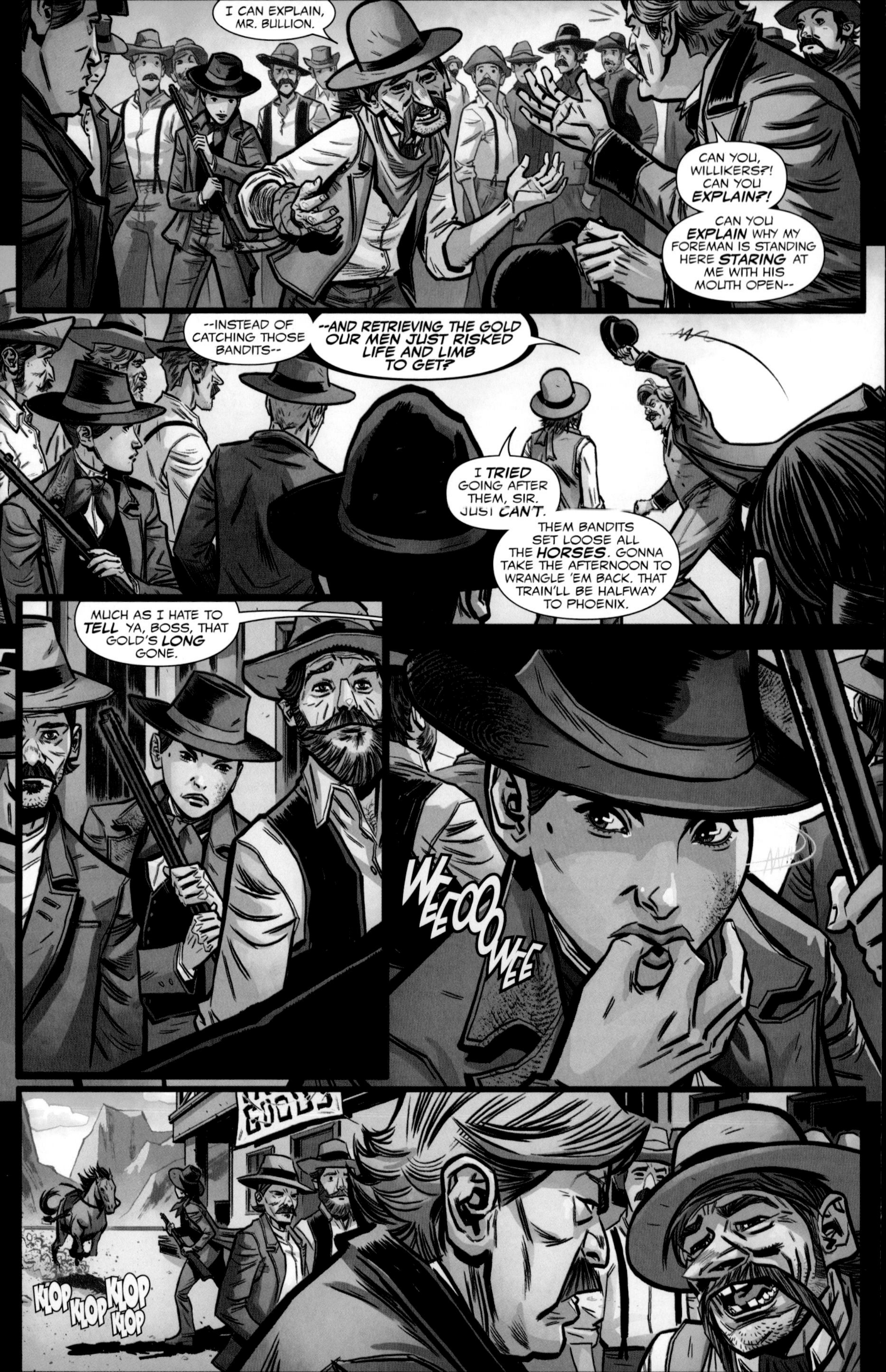
I CAN EXPLAIN, MR. BULLION.
CAN YOU, WILLIKERS?! CAN YOU EXPLAIN?!
CAN YOU EXPLAIN WHY MY FOREMAN IS STANDING HERE STARING AT ME WITH HIS MOUTH OPEN--
--INSTEAD OF CATCHING THOSE BANDITS--
--AND RETRIEVING THE GOLD OUR MEN JUST RISKED LIFE AND LIMB TO GET?
I TRIED GOING AFTER THEM, SIR. JUST CAN'T.
THEM BANDITS SET LOOSE ALL THE HORSES. GONNA TAKE THE AFTERNOON TO WRANGLE 'EM BACK. THAT TRAIN'LL BE HALFWAY TO PHOENIX.
MUCH AS I HATE TO TELL YA, BOSS, THAT GOLD'S LONG GONE.
WEEOOOWEE
GOODS
KLOP KLOP KLOP KLOP

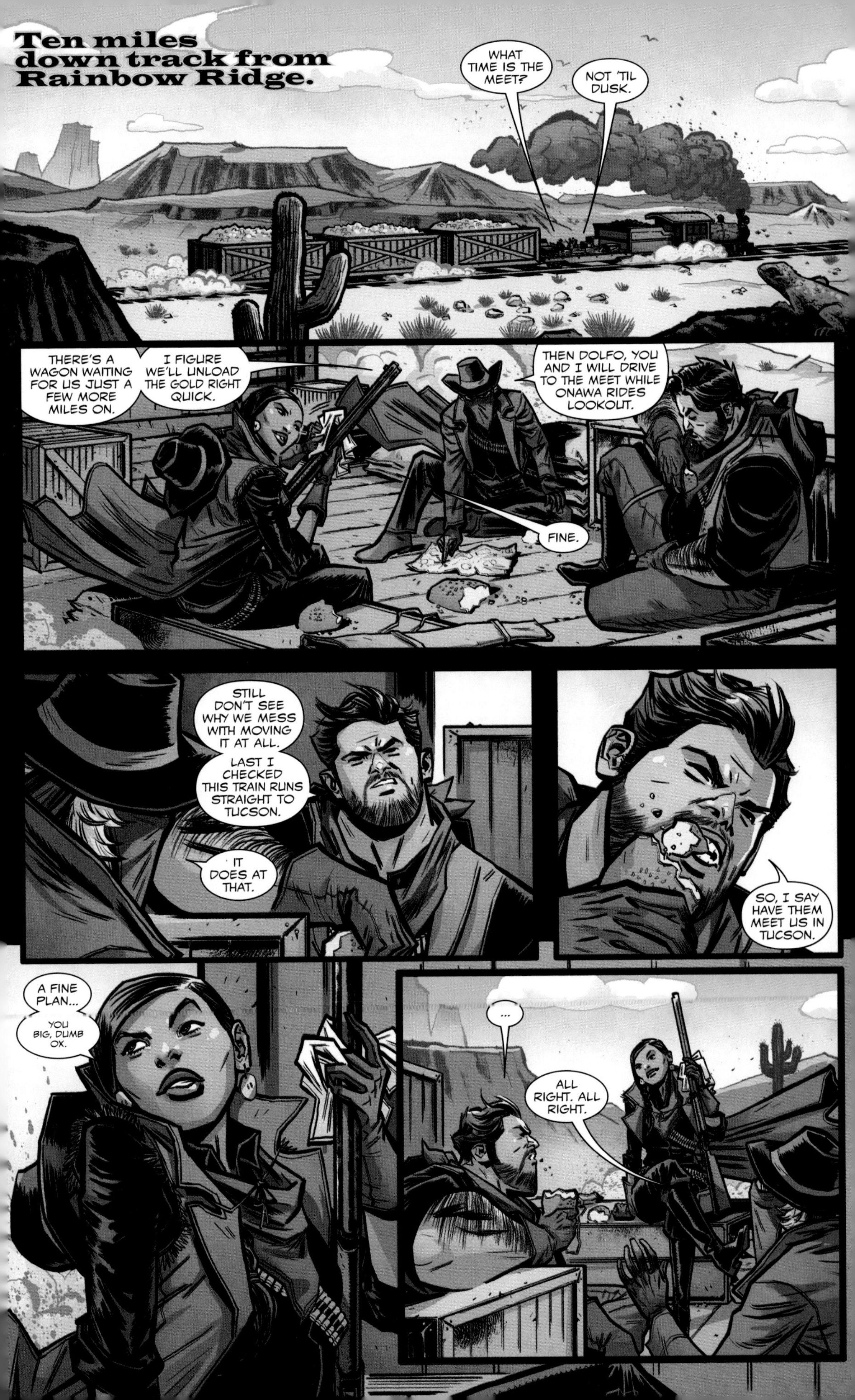
Ten miles down track from Rainbow Ridge.
WHAT TIME IS THE MEET?
NOT 'TIL DUSK.
THERE'S A WAGON WAITING FOR US JUST A FEW MORE MILES ON.
I FIGURE WE'LL UNLOAD THE GOLD RIGHT QUICK.
THEN DOLFO, YOU AND I WILL DRIVE TO THE MEET WHILE ONAWA RIDES LOOKOUT.
FINE.
STILL DON'T SEE WHY WE MESS WITH MOVING IT AT ALL.
LAST I CHECKED THIS TRAIN RUNS STRAIGHT TO TUCSON.
IT DOES AT THAT.
SO, I SAY HAVE THEM MEET US IN TUCSON.
A FINE PLAN...
YOU BIG, DUMB OX.
...
ALL RIGHT. ALL RIGHT.

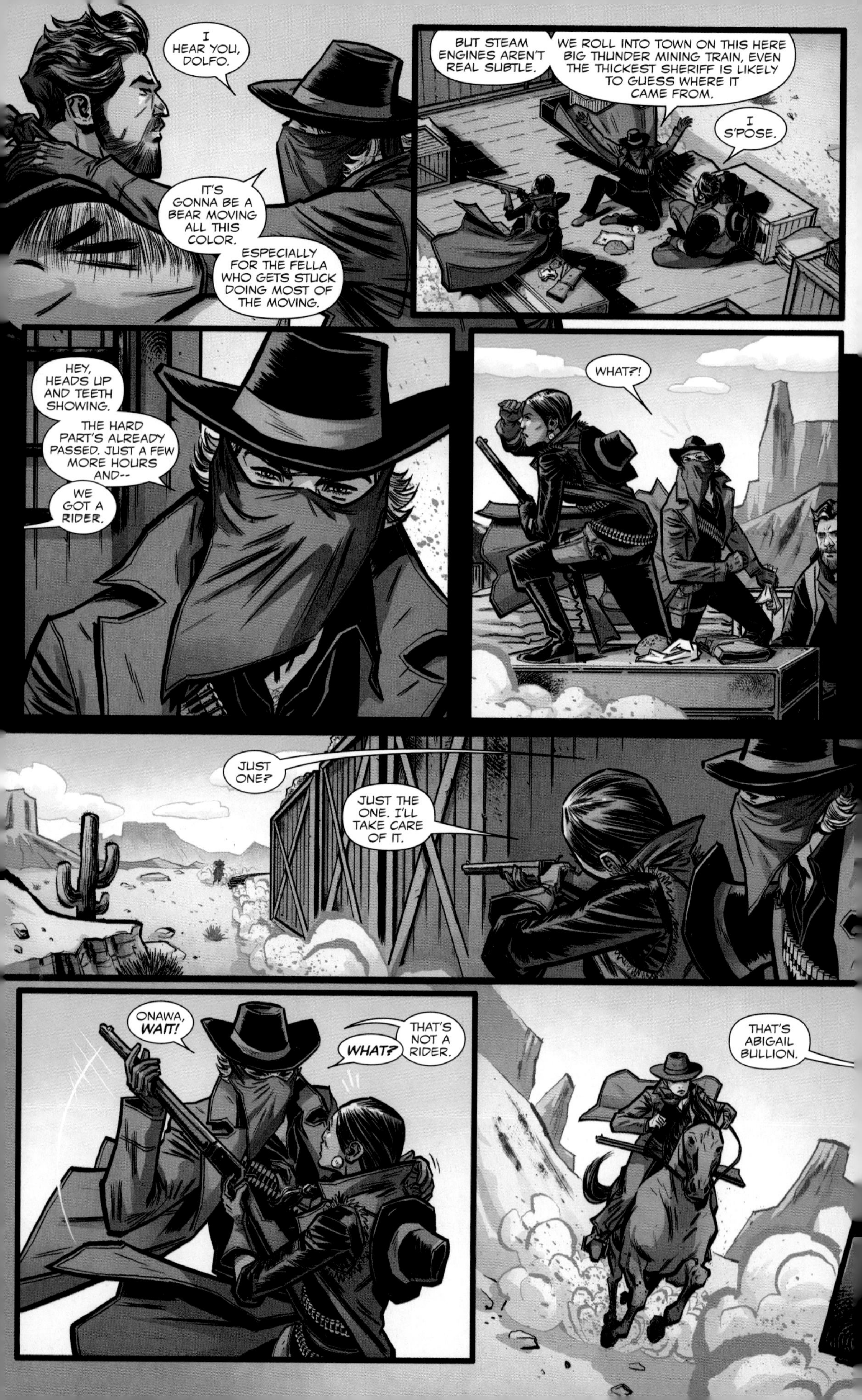
I HEAR YOU, DOLFO.
IT'S GONNA BE A BEAR MOVING ALL THIS COLOR.
ESPECIALLY FOR THE FELLA WHO GETS STUCK DOING MOST OF THE MOVING.
BUT STEAM ENGINES AREN'T REAL SUBTLE.
WE ROLL INTO TOWN ON THIS HERE BIG THUNDER MINING TRAIN, EVEN THE THICKEST SHERIFF IS LIKELY TO GUESS WHERE IT CAME FROM.
I S'POSE.
HEY, HEADS UP AND TEETH SHOWING.
THE HARD PART'S ALREADY PASSED. JUST A FEW MORE HOURS AND--
WE GOT A RIDER.
WHAT?!
JUST ONE?
JUST THE ONE. I'LL TAKE CARE OF IT.
ONAWA, WAIT!
THAT'S NOT A RIDER.
WHAT?
THAT'S ABIGAIL BULLION.

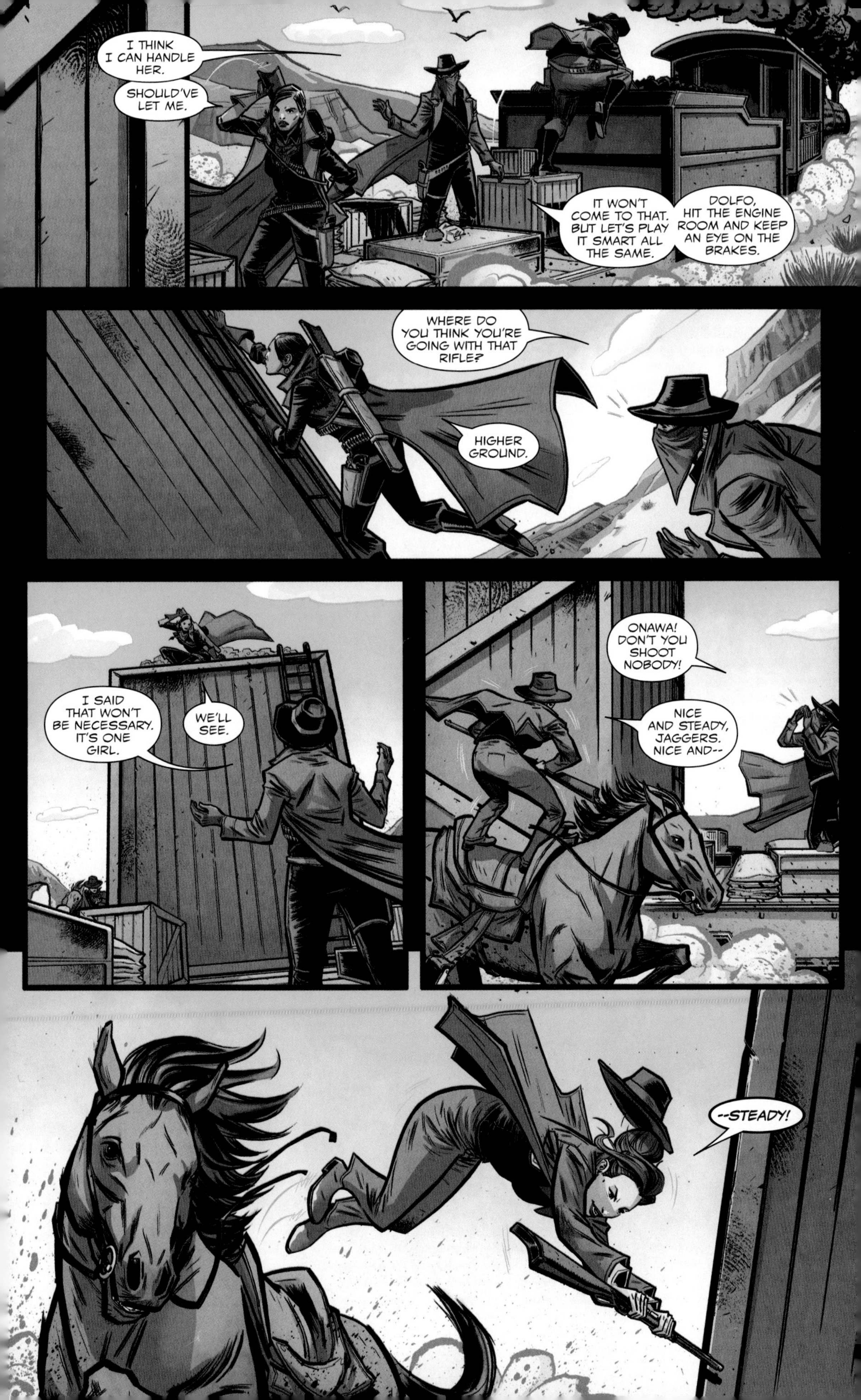
I THINK I CAN HANDLE HER.
SHOULD'VE LET ME.
IT WON'T COME TO THAT. BUT LET'S PLAY IT SMART ALL THE SAME.
DOLFO, HIT THE ENGINE ROOM AND KEEP AN EYE ON THE BRAKES.
WHERE DO YOU THINK YOU'RE GOING WITH THAT RIFLE?
HIGHER GROUND.
I SAID THAT WON'T BE NECESSARY. IT'S ONE GIRL.
WE'LL SEE.
ONAWA! DON'T YOU SHOOT NOBODY!
NICE AND STEADY, JAGGERS. NICE AND--
--STEADY!

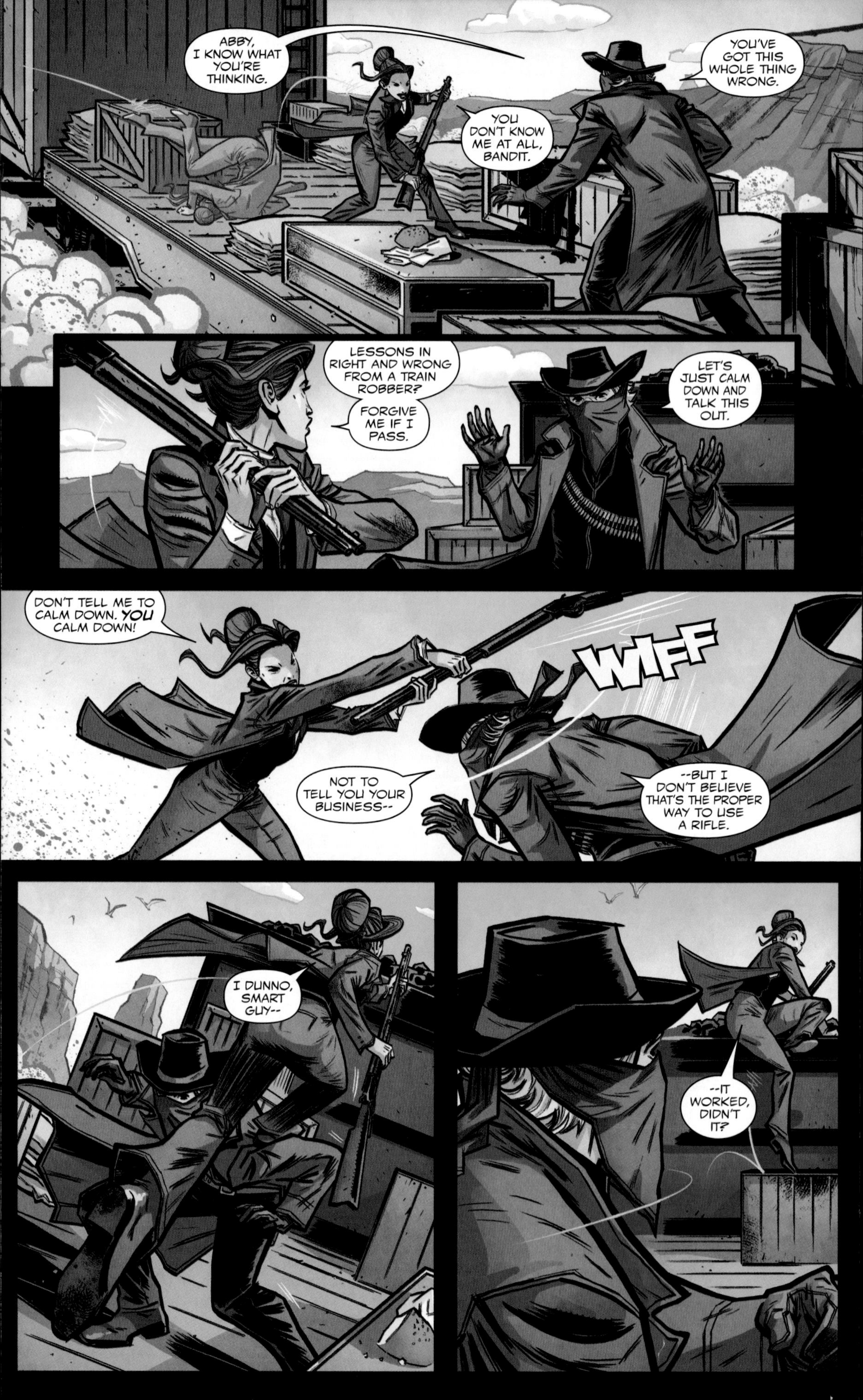
ABBY, I KNOW WHAT YOU'RE THINKING.
YOU'VE GOT THIS WHOLE THING WRONG.
YOU DON'T KNOW ME AT ALL, BANDIT.
LESSONS IN RIGHT AND WRONG FROM A TRAIN ROBBER?
FORGIVE ME IF I PASS.
LET'S JUST CALM DOWN AND TALK THIS OUT.
DON'T TELL ME TO CALM DOWN. YOU CALM DOWN!
WIFF
NOT TO TELL YOU YOUR BUSINESS--
--BUT I DON'T BELIEVE THAT'S THE PROPER WAY TO USE A RIFLE.
I DUNNO, SMART GUY--
--IT WORKED, DIDN'T IT?

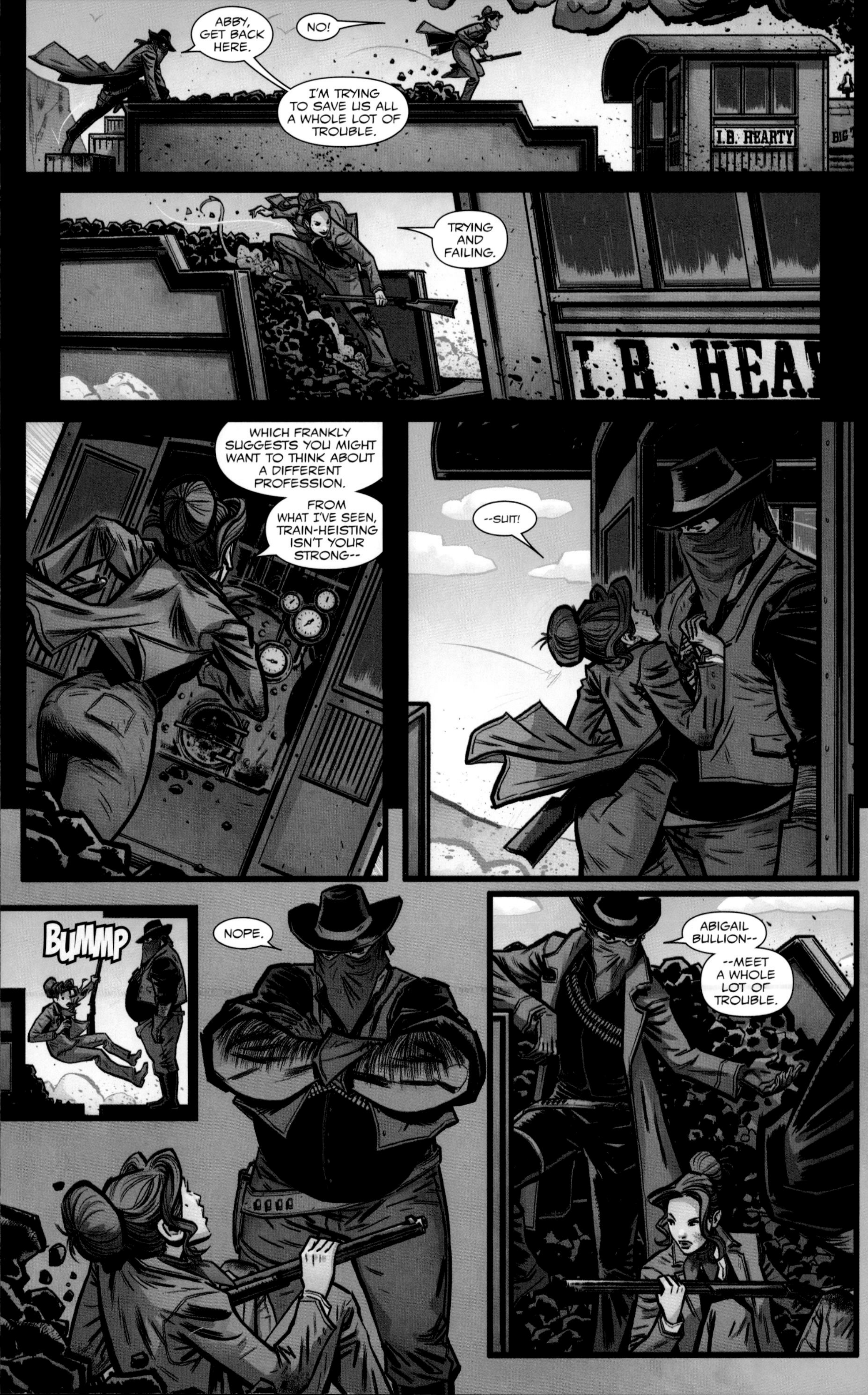
ABBY, GET BACK HERE.
NO!
I'M TRYING TO SAVE US ALL A WHOLE LOT OF TROUBLE.
I.B. HEARTY
TRYING AND FAILING.
WHICH FRANKLY SUGGESTS YOU MIGHT WANT TO THINK ABOUT A DIFFERENT PROFESSION.
FROM WHAT I'VE SEEN, TRAIN-HEISTING ISN'T YOUR STRONG--
--SUIT!
BUMMP
NOPE.
ABIGAIL BULLION--
--MEET A WHOLE LOT OF TROUBLE.

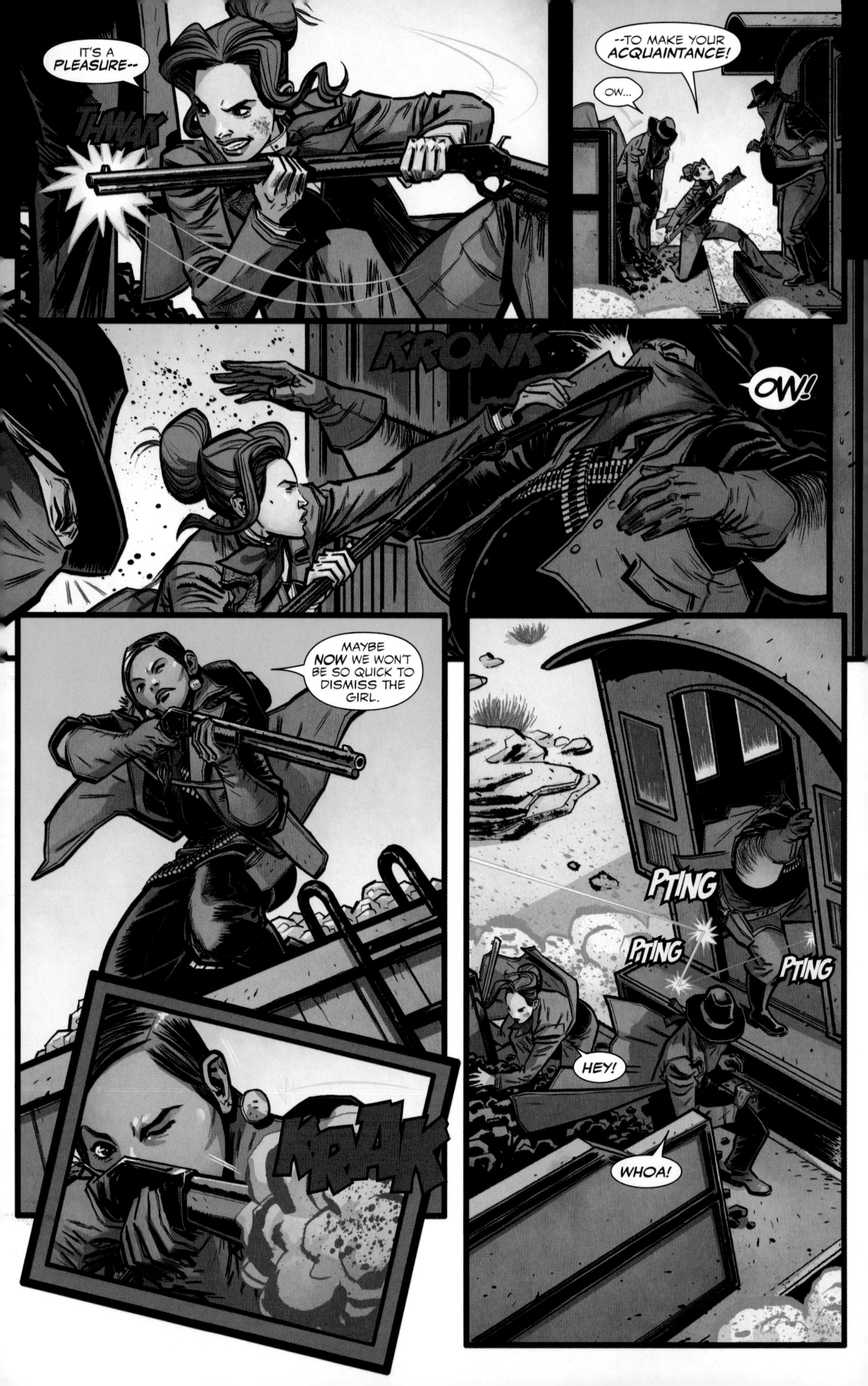
IT'S A PLEASURE--
THWAK
--TO MAKE YOUR ACQUAINTANCE!
OW...
KRONK
OW!
MAYBE NOW WE WON'T BE SO QUICK TO DISMISS THE GIRL.
KRAAK
PTING
PTING
PTING
HEY!
WHOA!

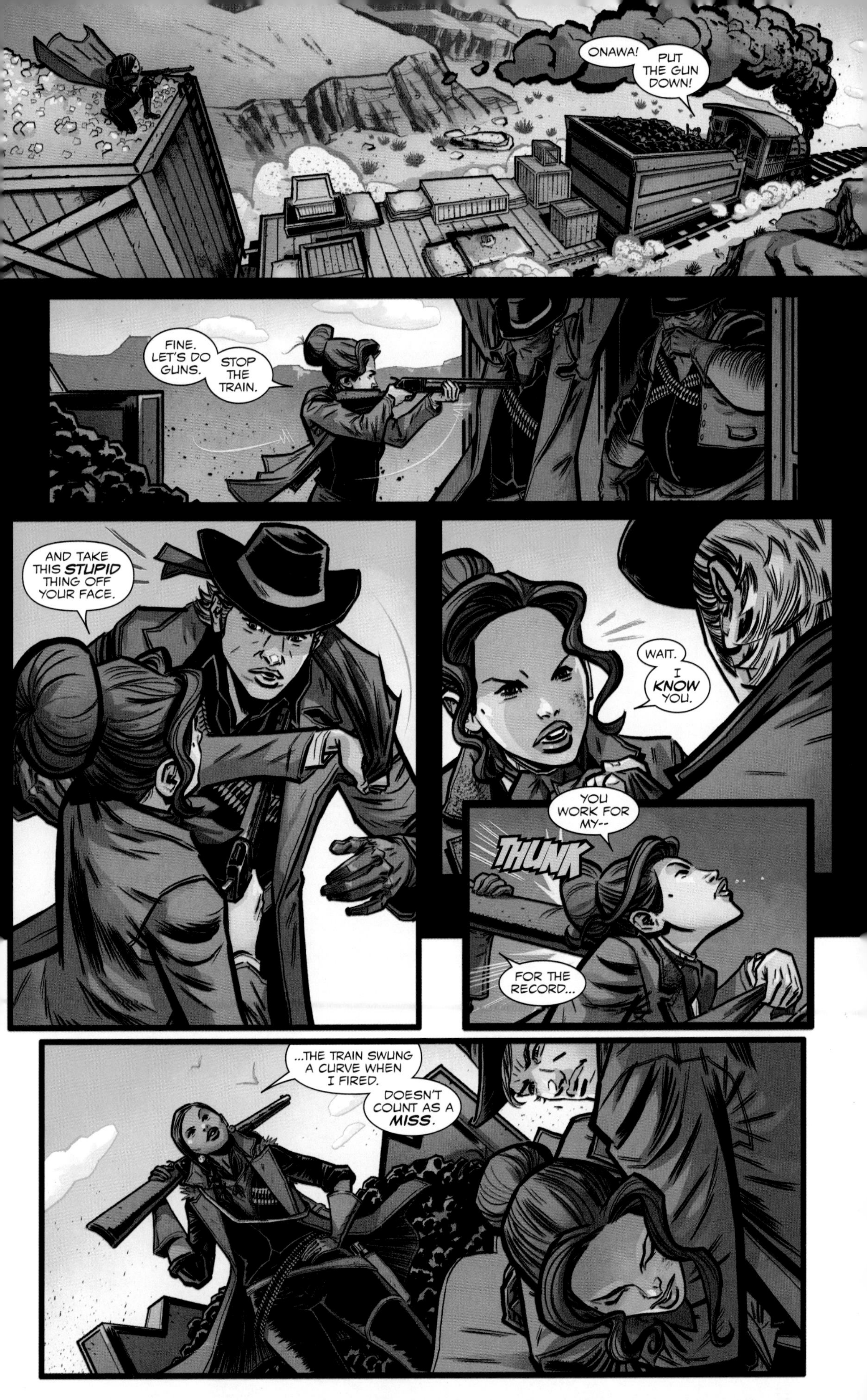
ONAWA!
PUT THE GUN DOWN!
FINE. LET'S DO GUNS.
STOP THE TRAIN.
AND TAKE THIS **STUPID** THING OFF YOUR FACE.
WAIT. I **KNOW** YOU.
YOU WORK FOR MY--
THUNK
FOR THE RECORD...
...THE TRAIN SWUNG A CURVE WHEN I FIRED.
DOESN'T COUNT AS A **MISS**.

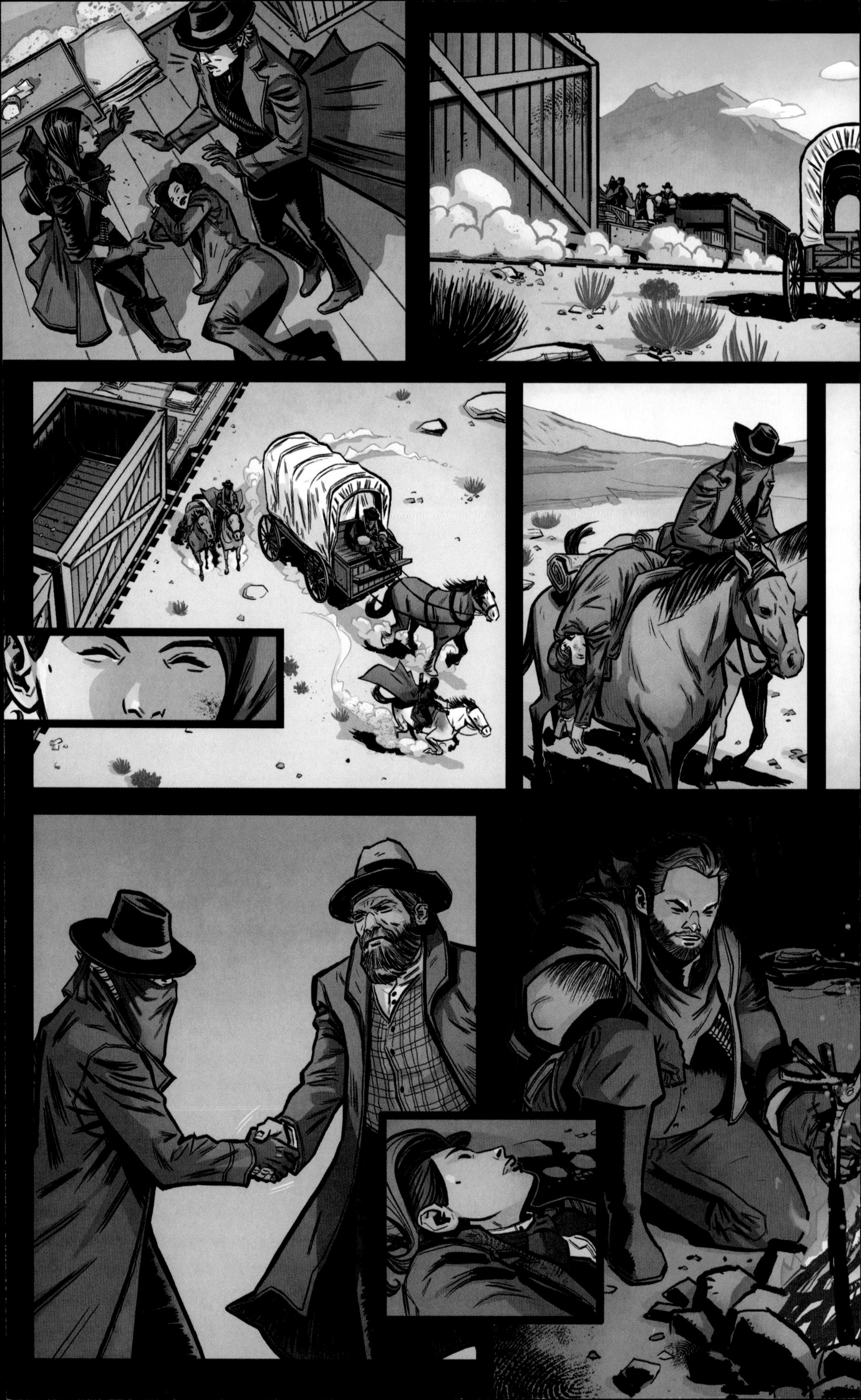

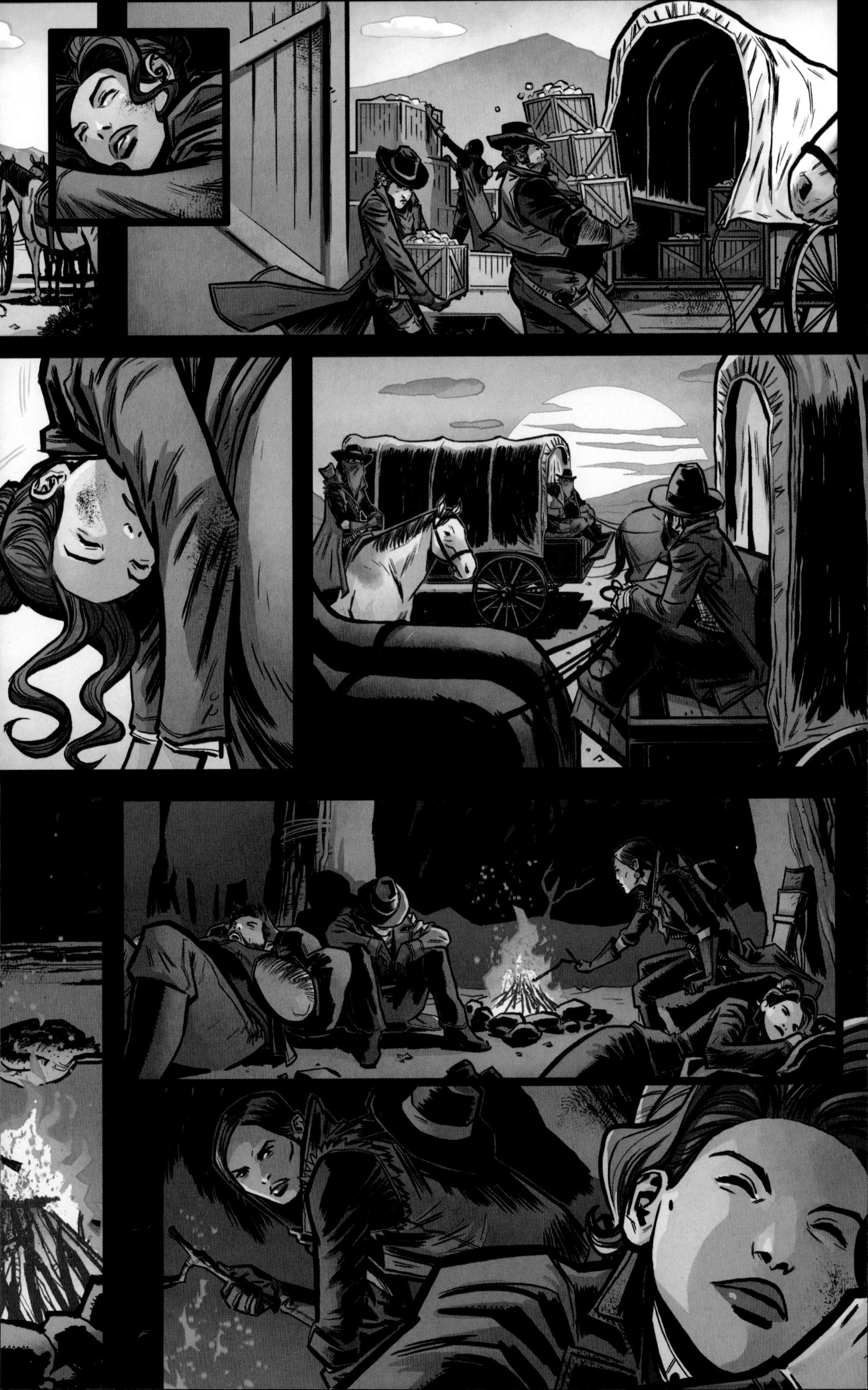

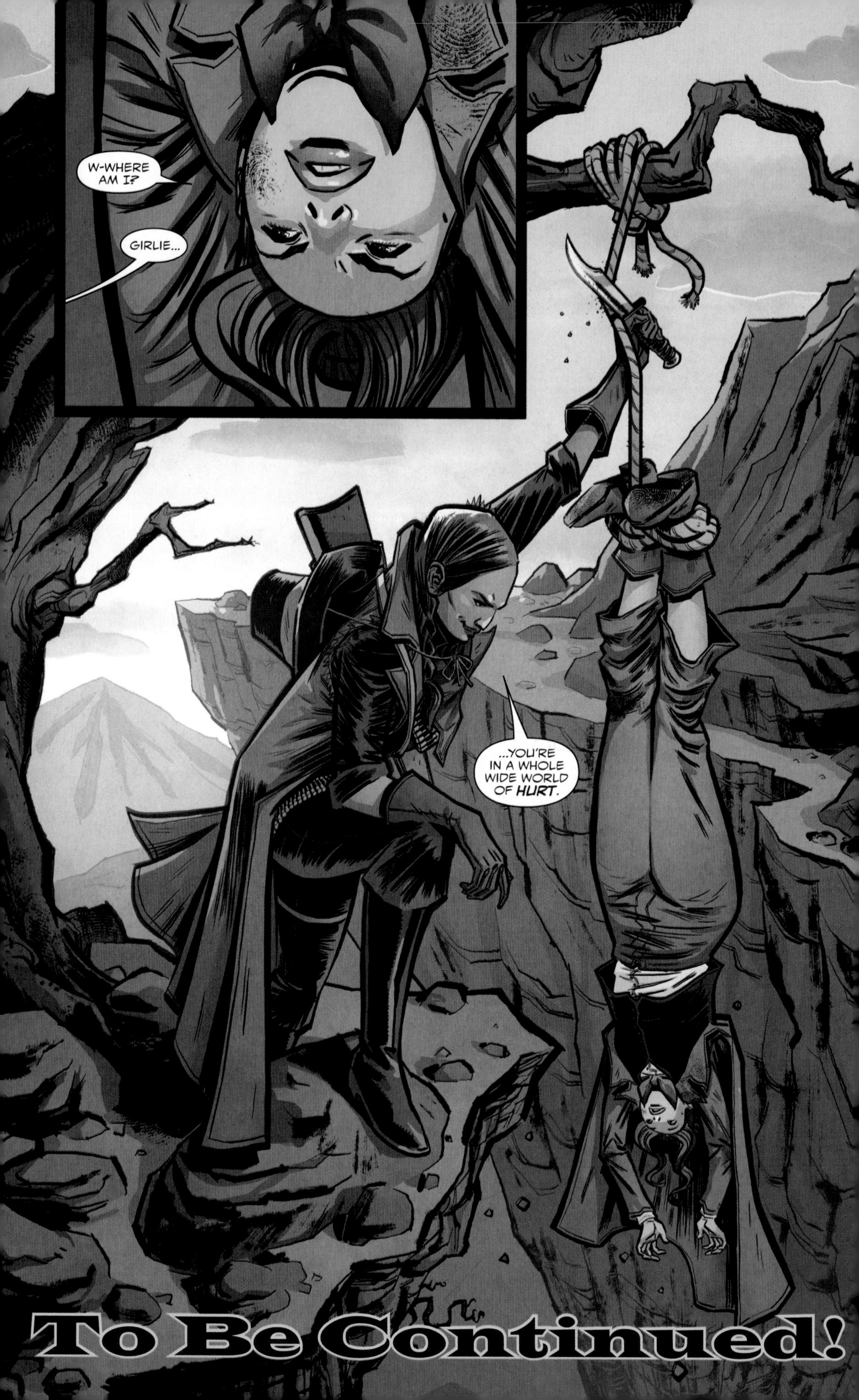
W-WHERE AM I?
GIRLIE...
...YOU'RE IN A WHOLE WIDE WORLD OF HURT.
To Be Continued!

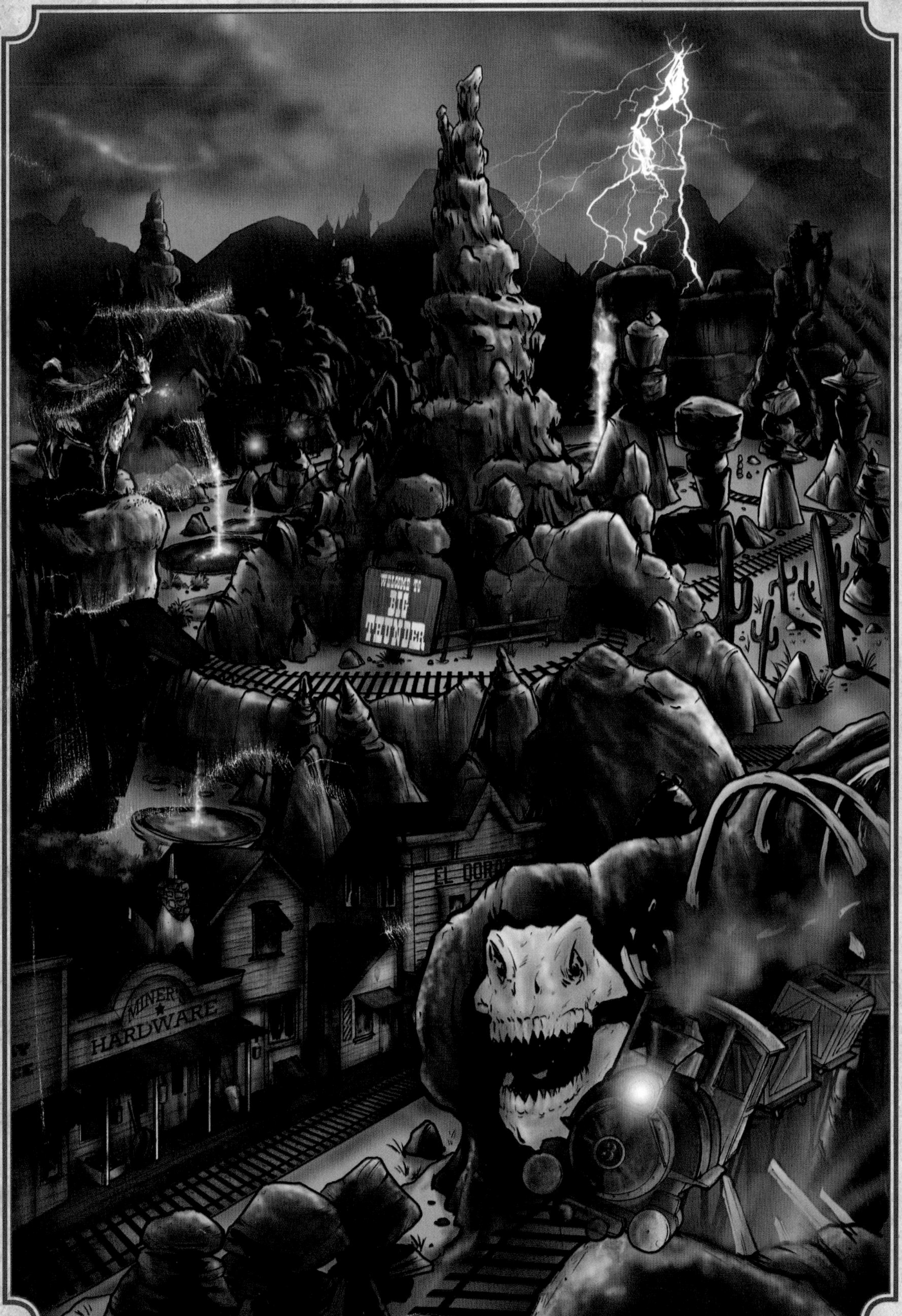
WELCOME TO
BIG
THUNDER
EL DORADO
MINER'S
HARDWARE

Big Thunder Mountain Railroad #1–4
Connecting Variant Covers by Brian Crosby

Disney KINGDOMS

BIG THUNDER MOUNTAIN RAILROAD

Disney KINGDOMS
BIG THUNDER
MOUNTAIN RAILROAD
MARVEL
HOPELESS
WALKER
BEAULIEU
#1

Hardcover Book ISBN
978-1-61479-575-9

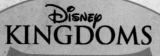

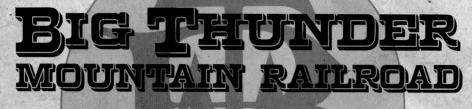

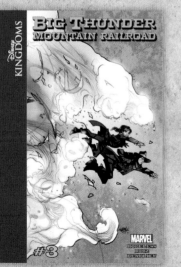

COLLECT THEM ALL!

Set of 5
Hardcover Books ISBN:
978-1-61479-574-2

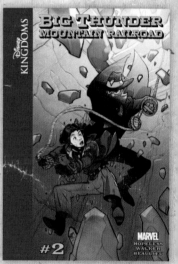

Disney KINGDOMS
BIG THUNDER
MOUNTAIN RAILROAD
MARVEL
HOPELESS
WALKER
BEAULIEU
#2

Hardcover Book ISBN
978-1-61479-576-6

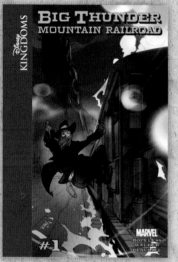

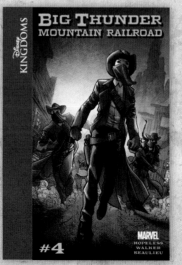

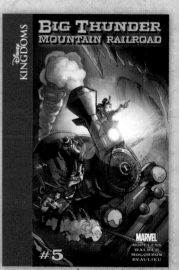

Disney KINGDOMS
BIG THUNDER
MOUNTAIN RAILROAD
MARVEL
#3

Hardcover Book ISBN
978-1-61479-577-3

Disney KINGDOMS
BIG THUNDER
MOUNTAIN RAILROAD
MARVEL
HOPELESS
WALKER
BEAULIEU
#4

Hardcover Book ISBN
978-1-61479-578-0

Disney KINGDOMS
BIG THUNDER
MOUNTAIN RAILROAD
MARVEL
HOPELESS
WALKER
MOGORRON
BEAULIEU
#5

Hardcover Book ISBN
978-1-61479-579-7